This book belongs to:

For Nigel, my husband. With love. X
K.S.

Sir Charlie Stinky Socks would like to donate 10% of the royalties from
the sale of this book to Naomi House Children's Hospice.

EGMONT
We bring stories to life

First published in Great Britain in 2014
by Egmont UK Limited
The Yellow Building, 1 Nicholas Road, London W11 4AN
www.egmont.co.uk

Text and illustrations copyright © Kristina Stephenson 2014

Kristina Stephenson has asserted her moral rights.

ISBN (HB) 978 14052 6809 7
ISBN (PB) 978 14052 6810 3

A CIP catalogue record for this book is available from the British Library.

THE PIRATE'S CURSE

Kristina Stephenson

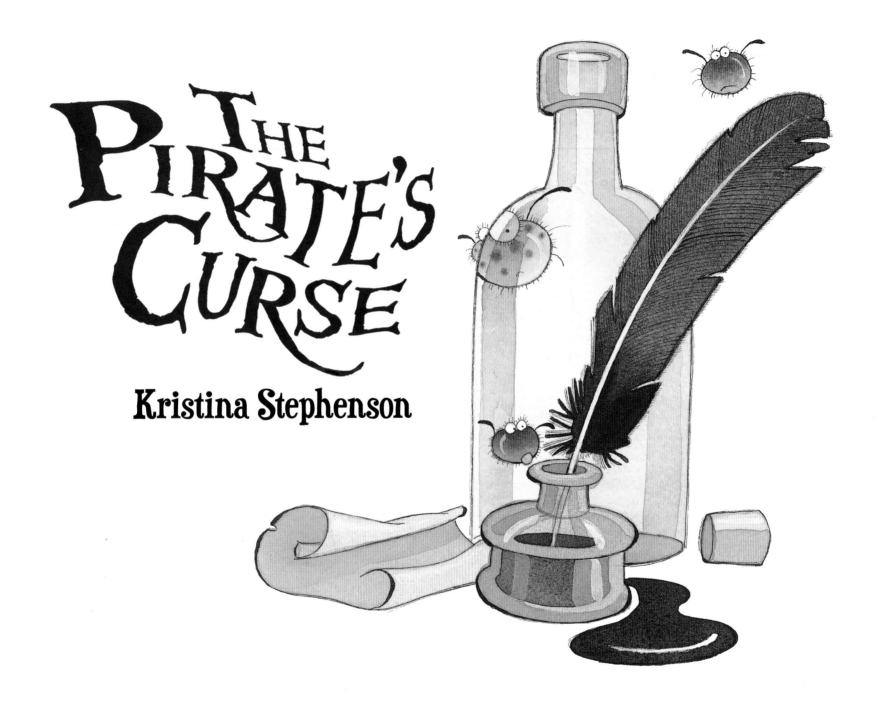

EGMONT

Once upon a time

there was a bottle bobbing,

out in the **big**

blue

sea . . .

a sea filled with **pirates** and *magical mermaids*.

Oh, and a **MAN-EATING MONSTER**!

The bottle went on bobbing for six long years without any sign of stopping.

More's the pity, for inside this bottle was a worrying little word . . .

HELP!

Shiver me timbers!

Splice the mainsail!

Someone was in trouble.

Oh my!

But never fear,
because land was near, and so was . . .

. . . a bold, brave knight!

Sir Charlie Stinky Socks,
his faithful cat, Envelope, and his good grey mare,
spotted the bottle bobbing in the water.

So they waded out to fetch it.

Splish-splash

splish-splash

splish-splash

Splosh!

"By jinkies!" said Sir Charlie, studying the note. "Someone at sea needs our help. Come on, my faithful, fearless friends, we need to find a ship."

And quicker than you could say, 'Watch out for **pirates**', they headed for adventure.

As luck would have it,
down in the harbour,
a ship was about to set sail.

A motley crew was raising the
gang plank and the captain
was holding the helm.

"Heave-ho, me horrible hearties!" he hollered.

Black

And the ship pulled away from the shore.

No time to ask permission to board;

just enough time to . . .

That fearless cat Envelope clung to the mainbrace.

So did the petrified mare!

For there, in the water, were sh . . . sh . . . sh . . . sharks *and* the cat and the horse couldn't swim.

But bold Sir Charlie
did not panic.

"Think again, captain," he said.

"Stowaways!"
shouted the **hairy-scary captain.** "Make 'em swim back to the shore."

Yikes!

Thump!

No one noticed the knight and his friends
as the ship sailed out to sea,

until a westerly wind
whipped up
a storm and . . .

**blew the
trio's cover.**

"For I am Sir Charlie Stinky Socks and
my stockings have a **mighty power**.

And consider my cat; not one rat
will bother you while *he's* here.

As for my horse;
my horse is, of course . . .

terribly good at . . .

ummm . . .

cleaning!"

Huh?

"If you let us stay," said Sir Charlie to the captain, "think how useful we'll be."

Lucky for the trio the **hairy-scary captain** was surprisingly quick to agree.

The wind grew stronger, thunder roared, but Sir Charlie
went on with his mission.
He was searching for someone
who needed his help;
whoever that someone might be.

Over the sea.

Whooshity-whoosh!

Bash!

Crash!

Smash!

The waves tossed the boat,
which *tipped* and dipped towards . . .

. . . **fishing**!

Well,
the pong

was so

strong

from those

powerful socks

it lured . . .

the *magical mermaids*.

Black To

They calmed the s

The sun was setting when the ship reached
an island in the middle of the **big** blue sea.

Leaving his cat and his horse hard at work,
Sir Charlie went ashore.

"I'll bet someone here wrote the note," he said.
And off he went to explore . . .

(not noticing the crew was doing this too).

The captain stayed in his cabin.

Pitter-patter, pitter-patter, up to a candle-lit tavern,
where Sir Charlie found the townsfolk telling **pirate** tales.

Arrrgh!

"Burnt Beard's the worst of the lot," said the landlord,
"because people say he is . . .

Cursed!

"Why else would his motley crew never see him after the sun goes down? He must be more terrifying than the **MAN-EATING MONSTER** when he's locked in his cabin at night.

This **hairy-scary pirate captain** with

a purple patch
on one eye, and . . .

a **picture of his ship,**
the Black Toenail,
painted on his . . ."

. . . the big **Black Toenail** was pulling away from the shore.

The **pirates** had all returned with their plunder. The captain was still in his cabin.

So bold, brave Sir Charlie Stinky Socks took a running . . .

leap

... on to the **Black Toenail** to warn his friends and keep them out of danger.

(Just in case the cursed captain should come out of his cabin that night).

Safe out of sight, the trusty trio sailed back out to sea.

The moon was up.
The sea was calm.

Nothing stirred until . . .

"MONSTER ahoy!"

came the cry from the crow's-nest,
and everyone turned to see . . .

But – dear oh dear –
no **MAN-EATING MONSTER**
would ever be scared
of *this* **pirate**.

"Not to worry!" said
Sir Charlie to the captain,
"*I've* got a better idea.

You MUST tell the crew what it is you do.
Then get them to fire up the cannons."

...he went on eating cake
from **Ye Olde Black Toenail** —

the captain's cake shop,
beside the **big** blue sea.

Ye Olde
Black Toenail

THE END

"Hooray for Captain Burnt Beard!"
cheered the motley crew, who were terribly glad
their talented captain didn't like being a **pirate** because . . .

we!" they said.

gardener."

air."

So, the **pirates** gave back the things they
had stolen and started life anew, on the little island
in the **big** blue sea, where all their dreams came true.

And the munching, crunching **MAN EATING MONSTER**? Well . . .

So, six years ago I put a message in a bottle and sent it out to sea, hoping that someone would come and help me.

Nobody ever did.

And that's why I'm **cursed** to be a **pirate** by day and a secret baker by night!

Mind you," smiled the captain as the fog cleared away . . .

... a flying

That night, by the light
of a silvery moon,
the **MONSTER** had ...

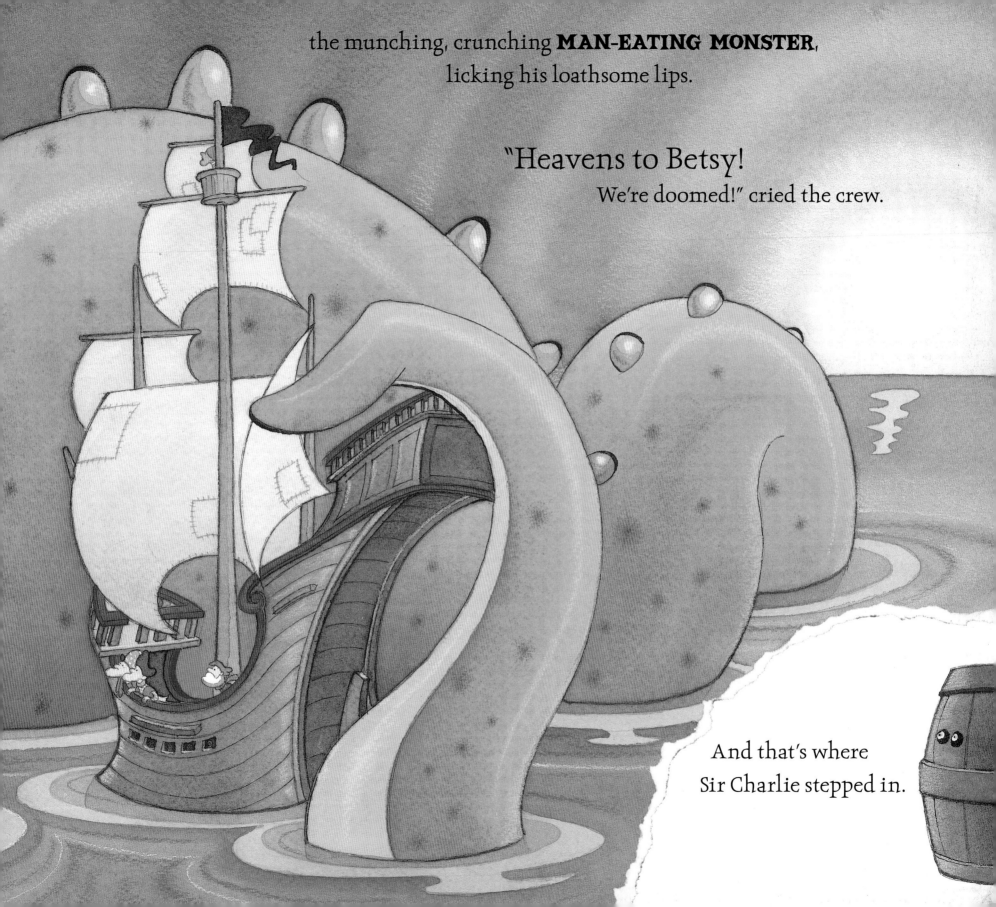

the munching, crunching **MAN-EATING MONSTER**,
licking his loathsome lips.

"Heavens to Betsy!
We're doomed!" cried the crew.

And that's where
Sir Charlie stepped in.

"Nonsense!" he said, popping out of the barrel, and remembering what the landlord had said.

"Go! Fetch your fearsome Captain Burnt Beard. The **MONSTER** will be **scared** of him."

But, so were the **pirates** (because of the curse).

'Twas up to the bold,
brave knight.

One quick flick
of his trusty sword opened
the captain's door, but not even
Sir Charlie Stinky Socks was
prepared for what he saw . . .

A fog of flour filled the room.

The captain was in the middle.

"I don't like being a **pirate**,"
he said.
"**I like** . . .

. . . **baking cakes!**

But I feared my crew would
laugh if they knew that
I burnt my beard
making muffins.